THE
ARTIST
WHO
PAINTED
A BLUE
HORSE

Homage to Franz Marc

Ann Beneduce, Consulting Editor

PUFFIN BOOKS Published by the Penguin Group: London, New York, Australia, Canada, India, Ireland, New Zealand and South Africa
Penguin Books Ltd, Registered Offices: 80 Strand, London WC2R 0RL, England
puffinbooks.com

First published in the USA by Philomel Books, a division of Penguin Young Readers Group, 2011
Published simultaneously in Great Britain in Puffin Books 2011
This edition published 2013
002

The text is set in 36-point Walbaum

The art was created with painted tissue-paper collage

Made and printed in China

ISBN: 978–0–141–34813–1

THE ARTIST WHO PAINTED A BLUE HORSE

by Eric Carle

PUFFIN

I am an artist

and I paint...

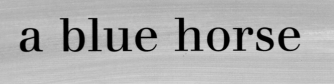

a blue horse

and...

a red crocodile

and...

a yellow cow

and...

a pink rabbit

and...

a green lion

and...

an orange elephant

and...

a purple fox

and...

a black polar bear

and...

a polka-dotted donkey.

I am a good artist.

Franz Marc, *Blue Horse I*, 1911. Städtische Galerie im Lenbachhaus, Munich, Germany.
Courtesy of SuperStock.

FRANZ MARC was born in Germany in 1880. He loved
to paint animals in bright and unusual colours. At the time,
some traditionalist critics objected to his new ideas and his
unconventional paintings, stylized in form and unrealistic in
colour. But Marc and some other like-minded artists formed
an art group that was highly influential in the modern and
expressionist movements. His paintings of blue horses are
particularly famous. Franz Marc was killed in the First World
War. In the pocket of his uniform was found a sketchbook
with thirty-six pencil drawings that, as he wrote to his wife,
he was planning to make into oil paintings upon his return.

ERIC CARLE was born in the United States of America
in 1929 but spent his boyhood in Germany. At that time,
the repressive Nazi regime forbade creating or displaying
modern, expressionistic or abstract art, which they called
"degenerate". But one day, when Eric was twelve or thirteen
years old, his art teacher, Herr Krauss, secretly showed
him some of the forbidden art. "I like the freedom and the
looseness in the way you draw and paint," he said, "but I am
only permitted to teach realistic art." And, pointing to the
reproductions, he went on: "Just look at the looseness, the
freedom and – ah! – the *beauty* of these paintings. The Nazis
have no idea what art is; they are charlatans!" At first young
Eric was shocked by the art and feared that Herr Krauss
had gone mad. Now Eric says, "My green lion, polka-dotted
donkey and other animals painted in the 'wrong' colours
were really born that day seventy years ago."

OTHER TITLES BY ERIC CARLE

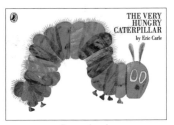

Paperback
9780140569322

Paperback
9780141332031

Paperback
9780140502848

Paperback
9780140506426

Paperback
9780140569896

Paperback
9780140509267

Paperback
9780140556780

Paperback
9780140569247

Paperback
9780140563788

Paperback
9780140557138

Paperback
9780140549270

Paperback
9780140562781

Paperback
9780140553109

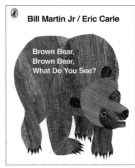

Paperback
9780141501598

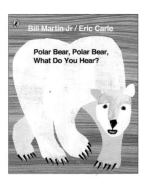

Paperback
9780141334813

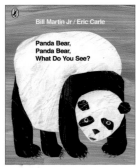

Paperback
9780141501451

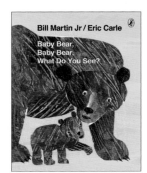

Paperback
9780141384450